Ava Vasileva was born in 1984 in Sofia, Bulgaria and went to France in her late 20s as a student. She teaches English to multicultural students in France and travels regularly to Bulgaria. Her stories are the fruit of experiences and observations from Bulgaria, France and beyond.

To Jerome

Ava Vasileva

TO BORROW A TULIP

AUSTIN MACAULEY PUBLISHERS™
LONDON • CAMBRIDGE • NEW YORK • SHARJAH

Copyright © Ava Vasileva 2024

The right of Ava Vasileva to be identified as author of this work has been asserted by the author in accordance with sections 77 and 78 of the Copyright, Designs and Patents Act 1988.

All rights reserved. No part of this publication may be reproduced, stored in a retrieval system or transmitted in any form or by any means, electronic, mechanical, photocopying, recording or otherwise, without the prior permission of the publishers.

Any person who commits any unauthorised act in relation to this publication may be liable to criminal prosecution and civil claims for damages.

This is a work of fiction. Names, characters, businesses, places, events, locales and incidents are either the products of the author's imagination or used in a fictitious manner. Any resemblance to actual persons, living or dead, or actual events is purely coincidental.

A CIP catalogue record for this title is available from the British Library.

ISBN 9781035821952 (Paperback)
ISBN 9781035821969 (ePub e-book)

www.austinmacauley.com

First Published 2024
Austin Macauley Publishers Ltd®
1 Canada Square
Canary Wharf
London
E14 5AA

I would like to thank Austin Macauley Publishers for their professional work on this book.

These stories are here thanks to people, experiences and coincidences. I express my gratitude for all of them. Some brought me love and pleasantness, and some gave me lessons and taught me to love. Or to write. And to love writing.

When it comes to people, I would certainly wish to say thanks to my dearest – some of them have been very encouraging, others less, but I love them all despite their weird ways. Thanks to my helpful friend who was always ready to help with reading or financing despite all her work. Thanks to my partner for his "No." when I asked "Do you like it?" after convincing him to read a new story, but also for his exclamations "I can't believe you wrote that! It's amazing!" (I don't know which sounds better.) Finally, I should mention P. S. for the urgent writing he provoked some years ago; had this affection been realisable, I might have not become a writer.

I could say so much more and mention everyone's name and the quality with which they have all helped so that these stories were created, but I just send them a thought of gratitude and let you carry on with the book.

Some of the stories came in moments of joy, and others came in times of distress, but of all the stages of the creation of this book, I enjoyed most writing them. I do hope that they will be enjoyed.

Table of Contents

The Woman in the Car	11
The Miracle Box	13
Avite and Helis	17
The Pens	22
The Fourth Cookie	25
The Wrinkles Around His Eyes	28
On Marriage or Something Like That	30
Nerium	36
Intrude Upon a Dream	39
A Block of Flats	49
To Borrow a Tulip	52

The Woman in the Car

I was driving my car and looking around. I especially enjoyed traffic jams, but not the ones on the motorway, rather the ones in town as I had the time to see the people and their faces.

The woman in the car behind was talking on the phone, hands free gadget I suppose. Her face looked stony, sharply drawn, her hair—like a well-groomed wig with a fringe but I guess it wasn't. I wondered what her story was. How did that face look before it became stony?

Her lips moved fast in little o-shapes and the wrinkles around them tried to catch up with the lips, as if with an effort.

Suddenly, the stony face stretched into a smile and some well-placed teeth showed up. There was a short instant when the stony face disappeared, and a young and vigorous woman shone behind the wheel.

Was she maybe like that other driver that I saw near Varna, with the big trembling earrings…She was moving her head to some music and singing with a wide-open mouth that would snap suddenly.

Only it looked like the same woman after the main events in her life had come and she had managed to handle them with the price of her juvenile softness. I wonder if she had been lucky to find the balance between confidence and humility.

I liked the one near Varna more; she looked like a juicy fruit full of self-assurance that bulged like the sugary droplet of a fig. She was wearing a straw hat over a glossy fringe. She was the kind of woman who didn't need a man to drive her anywhere.

The cars moved slowly and stopped again. The driver in the front was a man. The woman next to him was laughing, he seemed to be the reason for her laughter, she looked happy to be there. They were examining a piece of cardboard with arrows, a paper version of a GPS. She leaned towards him and kissed his cheek or somewhere between silky lips and scratchy beard. Blue eyes in the rear-view mirror.

Green lights.

She was the kind of woman who would let him press the pause button of her life.

The Miracle Box

Most of these places looked like little boxes full of washing machines. More boxes, with holes. People with their similar mindsets used to go to the *laverie* and wash their similar blankets and jeans. That's what I used to think anyway. They would put the laundry inside a little box with a window, add some coins, the lady with the curly hair literally added a two-euro coin in the washing powder compartment, press the green button, look at their phones while waiting and leave with a bag of washed clothes and sheets.

This place was clean and the music was nice; it made you want to dance. Tina Turner was shouting that we didn't need another hero and this improved my mood.

Dirty laundry, clean laundry.

Most people looked bored, waiting for clothes to become clean thanks to that magical little box with a window, that miraculous device that gave freedom to women. Though I usually observed that they didn't seem to be enjoying it properly. They would switch legs impatiently and scroll down the screens of their smartphones with no interest or engagement.

Today it felt different, being there felt worthwhile. One of the ladies was holding two cigarettes and caressing them in her palm. There was this slim young woman with curly hair, the one who dropped the money in the wrong place, she was knitting. It made me feel relaxed to look at her little fingers adding new lines to something that looked like a scarf. I felt as if I wanted to be with her until the yarn became a proper scarf, a long one.

My colourful t-shirts were going around the tumble dryer.

She went away without drying her clothes. I was going to recall this feeling of peace and try to imagine what the scarf would look like and who it was for.

Another woman came in. No greetings, fatigue and anger in her posture and her young face. A little child followed, sad and tired. She loaded the laundry and sat down, ignoring the boy deliberately. He was standing next to her chair, as if he didn't know how to approach her. She remained cold, her lips tight together. She looked furious at the boy, she let him stand for a long time without offering her lap. She stood, loaded the dryer and the little boy didn't take her seat although he looked exhausted. She sat down again and adjusted her mask, tears tried to find a way out. She looked at the child. That look reminded me of a parent I had seen once, smacking his child spitefully in front of the school and a moment later taking the child in his arms to comfort him. Only here it was happening in her mind. Her eyes closed; her chest raised; it was a prayer. As if she had kneeled down to ask her God to give her the right qualities and love to let her son grow well. She caressed the little cross on her necklace.

Then, her chest went down and it all went out with the air leaving her body. Her forehead became calm. She took off her mask to blow her nose in it.

The tumble dryer stopped. She took out a pile of sheets. Lavender scent.

Two women with Muslim clothes and scarves around their heads had entered, I hadn't noticed them. One of them was young and shiny and the other one was old and wrinkly. She was covered so well; I could only see a lot of deep wrinkles around her eyes.

The boy's mother tried to fold a sheet.

"Do you need some help?" the shiny Muslim suggested.

The mother nodded and a burst of tears let off. She cried like a child. The elderly Muslim woman took her in her arms. Her hands looked strong with labour, big and warm. She seemed to be the parent that this praying mother had needed so badly. The praying mother wept with relief and stayed in this healing embrace for a few moments. She explained later that she had little energy and she couldn't manage with the boy's tantrum. She had refused to buy what he had wanted in the shop and she didn't have anyone to help her with anything.

"I am a single mother, too. My son is five years old. This is my mother," said the shiny Muslim.

"My son is six and a half."

It felt like they were the only people in the *laverie*. There was me, of course, but I felt like one of the boxes with the windows, just an observer of a miracle.

The sheets were folded, mother and child took them to the car. Mother kneeled down and hugged the child.

The shiny Muslim followed and took out of her big, long gown the biggest and most colourful lollipop I had ever seen. Then she went back to the *laverie*.

"What shall we give them? What is the best thing that we have?" mother asked, looking in the shopping bags in the boot.

"Let's give them the figs."

Mother and child went back to the *laverie*, offered the figs and mother hugged the lady with the warmth and the wrinkles, crying and smiling at the same time.

"Thank you. May God protect you," the Muslim mother and daughter said.

"Thank you. May God protect you," answered the Christian mother and son.

I was putting my t-shirts and sheets in the car as if in slow motion.

Avite and Helis

For P. S.

Avite was reading 'Love in The Time of Cholera' for the first time. The book was still newly bought. She didn't know that she would be reading it for the third time eleven years later.

She felt her feet against the sand. If she stretched them, she felt its warmth, if she bent them—the coolness of the shade underneath the comfortable camping chair. She had just finished helping her father put up a big shade in front of the family camping home.

The neighbour with the caravan next-door, who couldn't help noticing her graceful movements and the delicate curves of her slender body, wondered why she didn't react to the constant criticism with which her father erupted. Now that she had helped a little, she could read her book in peace. She had also avoided conflict, so she was carefree.

Avite had spent the last fifteen years of her life trying to protect her parents from killing each other. She used the rest of her energy to get good marks at school and university. She was aware that most of her marks were not worth very much because she would forget the content as soon as the exam was over.

She was not conscious of her sexuality and not disturbed by it as she would be later. She was not conscious yet that she looked for intimate love as salvation.

Helis was dreaming of a farm. His favourite book as a boy used to be *Emil of Lönneberga*. He read it to his two-year-old daughter while his mother was making bread. The air in the living room was fresh but there was a light smell that resembled a basement in a village house, cheese, onions.

His hair had turned grey. Helis had just been gathering the courage to leave Enera when she told him she was expecting their daughter. He felt guilty and tried to live with her, as a good man was expected to do, but eventually listened to himself and left.

He discovered that this baby was not the end of his life, but rather, a new beginning. It felt like salvation when his daughter would lean her head on his chest and when covering her baby hand with his big, rough hand. It was comforting to protect someone.

But loneliness peeked at him and stifled his heart regularly. He had always imagined the love of his life in some ideal way. And had tried to find her in several women, most of whom had dark curly hair and a round face. But it never worked out properly. Either it was not possible for some reason, or he couldn't stand them eventually and wanted to be free and peaceful.

Avite was special for him and she liked mountains; it seemed promising. Perhaps she was the woman he had been waiting for all those years.

Avite knew that he was thinking of her. She would sense this when she was hundreds of kilometres away. She would sense it later when she was thousands of kilometres away.

She was sometimes too sure about him. She had the unwanted thought that she could flirt with the Australian caravan man and still be with Helis.

Later, in her thirties, she couldn't remember how she had fallen in love with Helis. She tried to recall and thought that she probably just felt ready to fall in love. It seemed to her that there were those moments when one needs romantic attention and they attract such. At that time, she received it from another man and this made her flourish, and right then Helis appeared, so he saw her glowing and vigorous. Still, why did *she* fall in love exactly with him? Oddly, it sometimes felt as if she had known him or seen him before, perhaps in her childhood. Occasionally, when she happened to be with people at important life-changing moments in her life, she would have this *déjà vu* impression that was both intriguing and disturbing.

Helis loved her enthusiasm. He needed her uplifting presence.

She finished the book in August and in September, she was already in his arms, her soft cheeks against his chest that felt like a warm rock.

She knew, however, that it was an escape for him from his daily responsibilities, and that she was stealing him for herself for just a little while. He wanted a family with Avite. He wanted a child from her.

She wanted him all for herself.

With time, she thought that life should be more than this. More than being with a favourite person in one place and sharing duties. Duties that did not feel hers.

She escaped from her dissatisfaction, from wanting and not getting what she wanted by choosing a literature adventure far from home.

He ached for her and thought that they might get married if he waited for her to become more mature.

***

A friend of hers loved her. She didn't want to disappoint him and slept with him. Helis was trying different women anyway and she was trying to let go of her attachment for him. She liked her friend after all.

Soon, Avite realised that she didn't really want to be with her foreign friend, but she didn't have the courage to tell him. She was expecting a baby.

***

Avite was reading 'Love in The Time of Cholera' for the second time, six years after the first reading by the sea observed by the caravan man. Florentino Ariza waited over fifty years to be with the woman he had chosen when he was eighteen. She identified herself with him. She imagined that she would wait for decades and eventually be with Helis.

***

She was reading 'Love in The Time of Cholera' for the third time, eleven years after the first reading by the sea. The doctor, the husband in the novel, was a very decent man, Avite thought. And he knew how to touch Fermina Daza. They could invent love, Marquez wrote. She associated the image of the kind doctor with that of her partner and co-parent and fell asleep with hope.

That night, she dreamt of Helis walking with her by a church. She woke up. She went to the toilet.

She went to bed again. Looked at the time on her phone. There was an email from Helis.

They hadn't seen each other for five years. She had woken up on other occasions during these years, after dreaming of him, surprised and frustrated that he was not next to her in the morning. She never said anything to anyone. Sometimes she wanted to cry but ignored the hollowness.

The subject of the email was 'dream'. He had a dream that they were walking together, and it felt real.

***

Six months later, they were standing together on the bridge in the provincial town near his farm. Cold autumn wind. Lights in the river. A man and a woman with grey hair.

The Pens

I was in that class that no one liked to work with. Our school was fine; they gave us free school bags and some pens and notebooks, this year they even gave us breakfast. I didn't like the pens, I preferred the four-colour pens I used to steal from the nice girls. The breakfast, however, was good, better than what I had at home. Sometimes I skipped breakfast at home and usually there was old bread with jam. I liked nuts the most, never had that at home.

I had two friends—one of them was like the nice girls, he helped me with homework sometimes. I know he didn't want to show up too much when I was in class, so he pretended that he knew less than he actually did. Honestly, I don't know why he did that. Anyway, I was often sent to the senior educational advisor, sounds like gobbledygook but it's the woman who threatens us with detention, exclusion from school and that sort of thing, so my smart friend could actually show all that he knew and get his good marks. Sometimes I wondered if I was doing it for him. Teachers had a lot of hope for him. (One of them had hope for me, too.)

The other one was useless at everything, it was amazing how useless he was, but teachers hated him because he would never react or respond to anything, *a-ny-thing*. So, that sometimes drove people crazier than my constant speaking to everyone in the middle of a lesson.

Well, sometimes I did other stuff to be sent away; I'd snap with my ruler and everyone would startle. I loved it, I enjoyed it and I'm wondering could it be crazy to enjoy annoying someone. I especially liked to see the furious facial expression of that perfect girl with the thick braid, who would cry, if you made a dot on her notebook. I didn't like to see her cry though, so I'd steel her pens delicately, so she always thought she'd lost them. And what's more, I mean plus the fun, the teachers wouldn't tolerate that type of disturbance more than three times (and that is for the patient ones), so they would get rid of me and give me my freedom. Well, it felt like this for some moments but then I'd be sent downstairs and sit with that woman with the marble eyes for the rest of the hour.

They would give me some text to copy ten times, so I would do this mechanically without thought and I would soon enjoy the calmness. I imagined that one day I'd give that braided classmate of mine all her missing pens and she would think I'm some sort of a hero. Or she would realise I'd stolen them and look at me with fury. I'm not sure which would give me more pleasure.

I haven't seen my father for two years now. I hate him. I know I should snap out of it, but I haven't been able so far.

Sometimes I hate my mum too. Last time I got punished at school, she exploded and slapped my face. Then she sent me to my room and I heard her cry for a long time. I wished that she would die.

Eventually, I felt that feeling of forgiveness that I had read about somewhere and fell asleep.

The next day, I wasn't angry at her anymore. I thought how funny it would be to make that patient teacher scream at me. Then I heard my mum speaking on the phone to someone, her voice was worried, thought I heard cancer. I asked, she said she had a breast cancer. She hugged me and said not to worry. I felt how my teeth were pressing hard against each other, I wanted them to crumble. (When I was small, they said I had a beautiful white smile but most blacks do.) As if my throat was pegged from the inside. I didn't cry, that would make her cancer spread all over her. I just nodded my head with agreement.

That day, I went to school and I said hello to the teacher whose skirt I had once lifted with the ruler to make the class laugh. I gave the pens to *Fury*. I didn't care what she thought. I didn't speak with anyone in class. Wishes come true then. But why so fast? I should have added 'in fifty years', she'd be ninety then. I continued imagining how I wish things will be in ten years, twenty years…

"Please, write."

Her operation would be successful. That's how I wanted to write it.

I would go and steal some nuts for her.

Maybe I could just ask for some nuts.

The bell rang.

The Fourth Cookie

Warm and delightful smell of baked bread and desserts made with flour. A cold autumn morning. Sleepy people rushing through the main streets of the small town. Raincoats.

A fountain with a statue. A woman in her fifties walking around the fountain aimlessly. Talking alone. Raising her voice. She has a white cotton hat.

A young woman passes by. Her heart sinks. The woman with the white hat looks like the young one passing by. The young one sees a resemblance and slows her pace, freezing with fear.

She goes into the bakery, tries to find a feeling of security in the warmth and cosiness of the place. She needs something for breakfast, maybe a thick cookie with nuts, it doesn't look oily. It must be tasty, she should get one for her child. Her partner likes hazelnuts, she'd better take three.

"Four cookies, please."

The fountain statue looks down at the little woman with the white hat, like a monster that punishes with indifference. The people who pass by seem unconcerned or relieved that they have a better life.

She runs and hands out the fourth cookie to the woman with the white hat.

And rushes off as fast as she can, unsure, a little afraid of any proximity, a little afraid of the woman but most of all anguished by the resemblance she sees, and the fear of the unknown. She weeps all the way to the university building where her young colleagues smoke and there is something effortless about them.

She goes home and writes three pages. She goes to the doctor. She goes to the psychotherapist.

It's spring. The fountain. The statue seems absent. The small shopping street that starts from the bakery. At the end of the street there are steps, then another statue-less fountain. She goes up these steps and a woman with a delicate face says, "Hello," and smiles. Her heart stops.

She answers back, "Hello," to the woman with the white cotton hat.

***

Three years later.

She sits in a comfortable armchair with a cushion behind the lower part of her back, moving her eyes left and right, following a bright green, soft ball on a metal stick that the therapist moves vigorously as if she sweeps something from dust. Thoughts appear and are swept away. This eye movement method is quite good. It helps the brain let go of the traumas and eventually a positive image appears and replaces trauma and fear.

The last image that popped in her head and remained there all the way, many years after she left that cushion behind her back, was the image of her in a colourful dress with roses, a separate and different person, who does not resemble the woman with the white hat but has the power to move statues.

The Wrinkles Around His Eyes

He went to the stable and the first thing he saw was the little lamb that was born last night. He couldn't get tired of babies, lambs, puppies, kittens. They were everywhere, he didn't feed them with expensive food but gave them all a little milk, a little bread; there was always place for a new arrival.

His third child arrived a year ago.

He caressed the sheep's head and then the little lamb, knees bent, knowing that he can't stay long because his students would soon be waiting for him in the town. As his rough fingers touched the softness of the wool, he smiled and wrinkled his nose for an instant. A little kitten rubbed against his ankle for attention. He picked it and laughed with delight, stroking its fur. The wrinkles around his eyes deepened with the wide smile.

He fed the kittens and left, walking with lightness, his always straight back; moved the tyre of the tractor, straining his strong but delicate muscles and washed his hands with cold water from the well.

He arrived cheerful in the kitchen where his daughter was disagreeing with her mother, who was warming milk for the baby and looking tired and cantankerous. He gave breakfast to his daughter and encouraged her to get ready. Went to get dressed.

He checked the roughness of his beard, moving his hands upward, opened his eyes widely in front of the mirror, tapping his temples gently as if to smooth the wrinkles around his eyes, regretting that he needs to do this. A melancholy ran through his mouth. Vitality seemed to go back to the stable. He went to the kitchen silent, rubbing his left arm. A sigh filled the kitchen.

"Did you sleep well?" he asked.

"No."

"What should I buy on the way back?"

"I'll send you a message."

"We must go." And he took his daughter's bag.

The steering wheel is cold, his fingers feel thinner, his skin—dryer, but he enjoys a getting-ready-for-work vigour and focus that improve his mood.

That evening he falls asleep during the pre-election campaign on TV and in his somnolence perceives the presence of the woman who kissed the wrinkles around his eyes ten years ago, when they were barely noticeable. His hand, resting empty on a cool pillow, feels touched. His face muscles relax. His breathing becomes steady, complete, calm.

On Marriage or Something Like That

She also could masturbate with clear conscience like her French friend, she had an interesting job and a salary that could pay the rent and the bills, drove her own car, could afford to get a dishwasher, so she didn't care about his habit of pulling away whenever he felt tired. This thought cooled the burning feeling in her throat while she was resisting her drowsiness, lying by his side in bed, wondering whether they would touch their shoulders. She had discovered the satisfying world of art and realised that sometimes she received from it a kind of satisfaction and calmness close to the bliss of shared love.

But there was one thing she couldn't do alone—stroke her hair. So, her ego softened and she fell asleep with relief, letting her hand rest in his dry, sinewy hand.

***

One day, he came back home, sat down in the kitchen and looked at her.

"I'm in love."

Obviously, he meant another woman or man or whatever but someone else. She started washing the dishes and there was only that vanilla-coloured plate that took all the space. She rinsed it six times, moving the flowing water in the plate with circular movements. It was pleasant.

He was somewhere behind observing her. He was wondering whether she would say something. It was enjoyable to expect her reaction, he would miss that if he left her.

The plates were washed. She thought about her saggy jeans and she supposed he thought how stooped she was while washing the dishes. The children passed by running, she smiled at them, wanted to be her best for them. She wouldn't have to think what *he* thought any more. She decided she wasn't going to wash his lunch box. She decided she wasn't going to wash the pans.

***

She did sulk for reasonable things and for utter nonsense. Especially the week before her monthly period she was even more sensitive. But sleeping together brought the best of both of them. Sleeping cleared her from her ego and in her slumber, she would embrace him. She perceived it as a good relationship in the morning.

Or he would find her beautiful with her curves and long hair and he would want to make love with her, so when he came to bed and saw her lying on her back with arms crossed, he would slowly get her to talk until they ended up laughing together. She thought he was great to be able to transform her mood like this.

But for some time, they had been sleeping in different rooms. Of course, he did this out of care for her, to avoid waking her up when he got up early for work although he woke her up anyway with his loud nose blowing. Sometimes he would wake her up during the night when he went to the toilet and then he would turn in bed. She would also move making sure it was as noisy as possible, so that he would know she was awake. They kept the door between the rooms open. She hoped he would do his gentle taming again. But recently, they had spent less and less time together.

***

She came out of her state of reduced sensibility and tried to understand how it had happened. Only a couple of weeks ago they were coming back from a Sunday outing, he was driving, the children were sleeping in the back, she covered his hand with hers, while he was waiting to change gears and he moved his thumb to lock her hand there for a couple of moments before he continued driving. She knew then that they were happy to be together.

***

Three weeks after abandoning the pans, after a shower, she felt calm and surprisingly, she felt free; liberated from expectations. It was such a delightful feeling of light-heartedness not to expect anything from him. He could no longer disappoint her in any way. She would scrub the toilet herself cheerfully instead of thinking that he never helped with this chore. If he were away and sounded cold on the phone, she wouldn't experience distress. After all, if his wish to live with her had faded away, it was better to leave her sooner than later.

She had a day just for herself (and some gardening and laundry). She was going to have lunch on her own, she liked it because she could even use the plate she'd used in the morning and left untouched on the table as if something had interrupted her breakfast. She could just take something simple, no fuss about a proper meal, no need to listen to anyone else's needs. It would be tomato, cucumber and crisps. And she would eat as much as she wanted from that packet of crisps.

She was taking in the shopping and taking off her shoes while searching for a forgotten thought. She had the intention to check something but forgot what. Some number...the time? No, the temperature. It was 23 degrees in the kitchen.

She went through half of the salad without realising that she was eating. Suddenly, she started feeling the taste of the vegetables and the sesame oil. She noticed that only half of the salad was on her vanilla plate, but she really enjoyed every fork of it. She thought that maybe it's the same with life— when you get sort of halfway, you start enjoying it more. The cucumbers were crunchy, never had she tasted such delicious and crunchy cucumbers. She was looking at the water from the tomatoes and discovering the difference of sensation in her mouth between the middle part of the crunchy cucumber and the peel, trying to define the texture and the aftertaste of each of them.

This took her to that summer before the children arrived in their life, when she was eating cucumber and tomato salad with cheese and soaking the oily tomato sauce on her plate with village bread. They had planned to spend a holiday together at her grandparents' house that used to be a hostel one hundred years ago. She usually conformed too much with everyone, so this time she wanted to be free, they would walk around naked and just listen to their wishes.

She closed the packet of crisps; they were very tasty; she must keep some for the children.

Anyway, that summer, he sat at the table and said cheerfully that his family wanted to visit the same village at the same time, so maybe she could accommodate them in her grandparents' house.

She laughed while folding the crisps packet. She didn't feel the old anger or the self-criticism that ate her then, after she had felt the anger. The family didn't come in the end and she was actually disappointed that they didn't come because she had programmed herself for their coming.

He could never understand this 'programming'. She tried to explain and asked him to read the chapter with the fox from 'The Little Prince' but he never read it. So, he tried to listen to her needs and make her happy without guidelines.

She always tried to do the same, sometimes it worked, sometimes it didn't.

In fact, often it was enough for her to feel that he was trying to listen to *her* needs, it changed everything. Her resistance could not exist anymore. She would let him lead.

She took a book and decided she would relax. She felt acceptance for this new challenge that he was giving her.

Yes, as soon as she had attuned herself to his new idea about something, he would speak and suggest something different, sometimes even exactly the same as she had been planning and expecting just before and that she had let go of.

Because she, too, was adapting to his wishes. Anyway, all this listening would be left in the past. Life could still be very nice.

That evening, he came back with the children and she wasn't even avoiding him. She embraced her new life that seemed already there. She smiled easily. After the children fell asleep, he approached her.

"We must speak. What's wrong? I'm not sure that you still want me."

She was looking at him and raising her left eyebrow higher and higher.

"I said that I'm in love with you and you suddenly became so…What's the word…And we haven't really spoken with each other all this time."

***

She fell asleep with a raised eyebrow and a smile.

Nerium

This story starts with the concrete pavement dusted with pink Nerium flowers from the clusters over a wall. Or better, it starts with the many pink flowers on the pavement. In fact, it also ends there.

On that same pavement there is a coffee shop. The chairs look dirty and sticky. Three little tables outside, just next to the street. A man is sitting at one of them. He wipes his moist forehead with the back of his hand. His face is naturally yellowish. It is shadowed by care.

There are two other men sitting at another table, playing a game and drinking mint tea in small glasses.

Cars stop at the traffic light and the air smells of their breath. It's eight in the morning but it's already hot.

A pregnant woman rushes on the opposite pavement. She has been walking from *gare Saint Antoine,* she has crossed *Rue Primitive* and now she is heading towards the bus stop. On the other side of the bus stop, an advertisement panel for an underwear shop frames the space. An enormous photo of a beautiful, dark-haired woman in a swimming suit, sitting on her knees. The photograph is taken slightly from the back or her right side, she is looking over her shoulder towards the camera and smiling. Her back is straight and wide, and her swimming suit has a surprisingly high cut and scarce fabric. One can remember this woman with her smooth white buttocks and her relaxed smile as if she is at ease with herself and the whole surrounding world. On the other side of the panel, there are two women wearing dark hijab dresses, waiting for the bus.

Two teenagers are playing a game with cards and dice on the bench at the bus stop.

"Five. What makes you happy?"

"I feel happy when I see my mum and when I eat," says the silky-haired teenager.

"How often do you see your mum?" asks the curly-haired teenager. Tight curls, pearly white teeth, fleshy lips and big eyes on a black face.

"Every day."

"That's lucky. My mum lives on our island with my brothers and sisters. I live here with a cousin. They sent me here to succeed. But I want to go home."

"It's your turn."

"Six. How many languages do you speak? I speak French and Comorian."

They get on the bus hastily and forget the die and one of the four cartons of the game. The pregnant woman sits on the bench and looks at the carton plate with the questions and the die. She touches the die as if she wants to throw it but pretends just to touch it. One. "Where do you live?" she reads in the first square of the carton.

At the railway station, she thinks, at the parking lot. Her cheerful mood and relaxed mind let displeasure purse her lips. Half an hour walking from this bus stop they lived in a caravan. Her husband defecated in the tunnel of the railway station. She asked in the Turkish shop, the lady let her use the toilet of the shop. She is getting used to it, but she wishes that she can tell this story using past tense. She waits for the bus which should take her somewhere better and then she will help her husband get a job. He is a good man although he drinks with the other Serbians at the parking lot. One of the others hits his wife when he gets drunk but not her husband; he only puts his arms around her neck and enjoys her like when they first met near Zlatibor, and forgets their reality. She loves him, she can't stand this parking lot, but she is getting used to the shit. She can't understand why they are here, but she follows him. She must find something. The Turkish lady tells her every day she must see a doctor. Maybe she should speak to the doctor. It can't be acceptable here in France to live without a toilet. It's unthinkable anywhere else.

She gets on the next bus and leaves the die on the bench.

On the way back, she gets off the bus on the opposite pavement. Her swollen feet step on the carpet of Nerium flowers. She stays there, the pink blossoms tickling her bare feet. The scent of the Nerium oleander uplifts her spirit. Hope spreads in her growing body.

Intrude Upon a Dream

Branimir was sitting, half-lying on the single bed in his favourite room. Two comfortable pillows behind his back. The house was a Bulgarian-Renaissance wooden house tucked in the folds of *Stara Planina*. A light breeze was swaying the vine leaves above the table on the terrace.

His favourite room was this one, it was planned as an 'office' although this house and the word 'office' were incongruous. He was looking at the window from his bed. There was a desk by the wall and the window was on the right side of the desk. It would have been convenient if he were left-handed, but he wasn't, so he had the idea of moving the desk on the right side of the window. He would finally get proper light on his books and papers. He was wondering what to put on the left side, once the desk was moved. He could build a shelf there or move the cupboard with the television. Or just throw out the television and make this shelf. He was fed up with the war, it sometimes felt as if he were carrying the weight of the whole world when he watched the news too often. During the covid story, it had felt as if all those people with masks were intruding in his bedroom. Because his favourite room with the wooden desk had become his *bedroom*.

Was it after the first child or after the second? The left corner of his lips moved into a slight smile that came with a snort, almost a beginning of laughter that stopped before it began. He thought, if they have the second child, they must have slept together before that. He didn't remember these things anymore. The/their bedroom was overcrowded. He found comfort and space in this room. And now his ideas were flowing even more freely because his wife and the children had gone for a few weeks to her parents' town.

He enjoyed the smell of the linden trees and the breeze through the open window. Moved the TV in that corner, then unplugged it and took it out. He felt light. He felt young. He sat and put his elbow on the newly-moved desk. He remembered a photograph he had taken of another woman so many years ago that he wasn't sure how many. He had taken this picture while she was walking along a sandy path between some marsh and the beach near *Durankulak*. On that photo, the scarf served her as a skirt; the wind was blowing it and he had thought that her ankles were beautiful. Now he only remembered a sketch of black hair, a sun-tanned back and a blue stain for the skirt. He wanted to see her right now, immediately.

He didn't like taking photos, so the few they had were precious and seemed exquisite, but he didn't remember whether he had kept this one.

They spoke once or twice a year. It had taken them some fifteen years for each of them to find their place in life without the other. They felt relieved of the old longing and had become friends eventually.

***

Divna was very cheerful this afternoon. Her boyfriend's mother had invited her to go with him this summer. She would probably meet her at last. She felt warm feelings for his mother because she hoped that it was partly her being a good mother that had made him a noble man. Divna also thought that she would at last get to have a more complete view of his world. It had felt to her so far that not seeing his family and his landmarks was like walking with an eye-patch on one eye, although both eyes were healthy.

She felt like dancing, put the speakers up and performed something like a contemporary dance in the living room.

She was imagining weddings and babies although she didn't intend to have babies.

At that moment, Branimir called, she tried to answer by sweeping the screen in the right direction but it didn't work and missed the call. She was the kind of person who would wonder whether she should leave it if the phone doesn't work the first time, but thought she should be more reasonable than that and simply called back.

So, they spoke of this and that, it was easy like with a real friend. They told each other of their respective gardens, and she explained how she had abandoned her boyfriend's beans when he hadn't been present enough. And she really only cared for the vegetables that could make a good *shopska salata*.

He suggested they meet one of the three days when he would be in her family's town.

She said she had a very busy schedule for the summer holiday, but she would be at the same place as him during those three days and they could have a lemonade together. He suggested a trip to that sandy path by the sea. And staying overnight by the seaside.

"Listen," she said, "if you can tell everyone that we are going on a one-day excursion and not cause ourselves a headache, I don't mind."

"Then, let's stay with the lemonade, otherwise we will probably cause ourselves a headache," he said, "but know that I will go to that place anyway." The way he pronounced 'headache' sounded flirty.

"But then, I feel as if I will miss something. Okay then, plan maximum—I join you; plan minimum—we just have a lemonade together."

It was three years ago when they last met, before she fell in love with her boyfriend, but things were different then. She had been waiting for Branimir for ten years and wanted him; he was almost divorced and as she was free, and he was not actually living with his wife, they made love and ate stretchy bakery-made *banitsa* for breakfast.

She wanted to see him without headaches now.

She imagined him stretching his feet (that never smelled) on that single bed, because they both knew a lot about each other's life and she knew that he slept alone. She thought of the posture of his slim and dry body and how he enjoyed thinking of her while his wife was away from home. There was something Divna didn't like about it, his enjoyment in thinking of her and not mentioning anything to his wife. This peace that he would maintain around himself by not opening too much to his wife. She thought that she understood why he always marvelled at her offhanded honesty.

She imagined herself in his car on the way to that camping near the nature reserve with all those protected species of birds. She would look at him and tell him that this time her heart was not free for him.

After the conversation, she climbed up the steps on the way to the forest in her village and felt comfortable and fresh with her hair up. Then imagined that when they met, she would wear her hair relaxed and not in a bun because she knew that he found her more beautiful this way. She observed with interest the thought that she wanted to be beautiful for him.

She had dinner with the neighbours and felt good about her boyfriend calling her every day while he was away for work. She felt carefree.

But that night, she dreamt of some lost keys and that she spent the night with Branimir.

Divna had forgotten the dream before she woke up and in the morning was rushing to write to her boyfriend. However, later she caught herself thinking what clothes she would wear when she met Branimir. That day, as she was going through some home magazines, she stopped on a page to enjoy a cosy room with an icon on a wooden wall and imagined that she had damaged the icon. A feeling of guilt was manifesting itself. So, she called her boyfriend and told him about the image of herself with free-flowing hair, the clothes and the flow of thoughts that she hadn't controlled.

Despite these reactions, she hoped that this time it would be different, a passionless friendship. When she thought of their bodies, she saw them as flat wooden planks, not the previous lust. Still, a friendship that she needed to keep, that she couldn't erase like her boyfriend wanted in a moment of panic, although he knew that she would only choose to love him if she was free. She knew that her boyfriend's dark mood after her extemporaneous confession of thoughts, was a good sign which meant she was important to him and she appreciated this.

***

Branimir and Divna will actually meet in four days. The omniscient narrator doesn't know whether they will walk together that sandy path from the old photo or they will just drink lemonade in town. He doesn't know what thoughts they will observe and if there will be any surprises.

***

First night: no dreams.

She walks down from the forest and an idea of white cherries knits a row of thoughts. "He wants me to freeze some white cherries so that he can taste them when he comes back from his trip, he said forty; how about 90…sounds like old age…Do I want to live until 90, he wants to live until 100, so I should be fine with 95…then I will pick 95 white cherries for him…If I live just a little shorter than him, I will not have to miss him…"

***

Second night's dream: *she puts on make-up; she is in a relationship with Branimir, there is a winding path, two separate gardens—one is hers and one is his; they argue as soon as they try to work together on a common garden.*

She wakes up, she doesn't remember her dream. Her first thought is of a baby with her boyfriend. She doesn't want a baby, but she feels grateful for this man.

She brushes her pearly even teeth and the image of her in a new dress pops up—she is going out of her parents' home to meet Branimir, he has come to pick her up like in the old times, so many years ago.

She walks along the aisles of the supermarket and near the shower items she thinks of her boyfriend, when they had a shower together, how handsome he was, how caring he was when she was being playful. Where does he get this nobleness from? Is she giving him qualities that he does not possess?

Later she thinks that she wants to talk and walk with Branimir and spend some time in peaceful silence with him. And just observe.

She excuses herself by explaining to herself that she does not feel like kissing him on the mouth (she checks again whether this is true and then continues with her excuses in the flow of this internal monologue); she imagines telling her boyfriend that she does not wish to make love to Branimir but she wants to walk this path with him for a day. Yet, in the evening when her boyfriend calls, she chooses not to talk about this because she prefers to keep the nice ambience (and because she wants her boyfriend to continue calling and opening up, and his voice has become lovelier since he misses her, and she doesn't want to change this). The conversation is interrupted anyway, bad connection. She remembers her criticism towards Branimir's secrecy and once again she confirms to herself that whenever you criticise someone, you get into a situation that makes you understand them.

***

Third night: no dreams.

A call from Branimir. His intonations resemble her boyfriend's intonations.

Quiet introspection.

Something rises in her chest and goes out as tears. This disturbs her and makes her dive deeper inside herself, she is simulating possible situations and checking how she would feel. She realises that if she follows Branimir in his new freedom, she will find herself again in a position she happened to be in some years ago when she was with a man she didn't love while thinking of Branimir. This time she would love the man as he would be Branimir but she would think of her boyfriend with whom she has been happy. She would have to live with a feeling of having lost someone and there would be a simultaneous life with him going on in her head for long enough to spoil a possible new beginning with Branimir. She feels grateful that she can see this.

Yet, she starts the car with determination. She can't wait for another day. She wants to meet him immediately and check what she feels. She will go to his place. It's like waiting for an exam in front of the professor's study; she wants to be the first to enter and relax after that.

Her reason for going three years ago was to start a new life with him.

Her reason for going now is to pay tribute to this love and let go. She wants this meeting to make the present more tangible, to bring her to the present day where Life is calling for her.

For him, it seems different. It seems that finally he is taking the courage to leave the unsatisfying relationship with his wife. He simply feels that it has ended tacitly. Yet, he is unsure whether they should meet at all. If he finds out that he wants her very much, this might turn his established world upside down. He also feels apprehension—what if they feel indifferent to each other; what if the magic isn't there anymore or vanishes during this meeting? This would make him feel empty and drained of the tickling force of love.

She thinks that she wants to see him with friendly love, but she is worried that she might find more than this. She worries just as much about finding less because this would humiliate him in her eyes.

***

She stops the car in Veliko Tarnovo and spends the night there. She can continue tomorrow, if she still wants to continue.

Fourth night: *someone is about to put a ring on her hand,* but she wakes up and hasn't seen his face.

She looks out of the window and sees a red rose bush. She thinks of her boyfriend. She didn't dare call him last night.

She decides to go back to sleep hoping to see the face of that man in her dream. She wonders who decides these things in life; falls asleep.

She dreams that she is with Branimir but she is wearing uncomfortable flip-flops.

***

Divna was woken up late by the smell of fried *mekitsi*. She had a cup of local tea, which warmed the morning air with Balkan herbs. The roses were shaking off the dew. The plump lady of the house brought fluffy *mekitsi* with blueberry jam and feta cheese. Divna moved all the delights, sat in the sun and enjoyed the right balance of crispiness and softness of the *mekitsi*. The blueberry jam changed the colour of her lips. Why did she have the idea of coming to Veliko Tarnovo, she couldn't say, but decided to go and visit the fortress.

A Block of Flats

Two youngsters sitting on the steps (three steps) in front of an ordinary building in Tallinn. Casual clothes, sport sandals. A backpack with a bottle of water, a few banknotes and two phones. A backpack to be filled with new onion, tomatoes, greens.

It's early and all the shops are closed. He says that they have half an hour to wait.

She is radiant with joy. Looks at him expecting to receive a look that she will interpret as a loving one. He thinks of the bus schedules and how the clocks are not set at the same time.

She is looking at the building just in front, a grey block of flats with terraces large enough for a table and three chairs but probably not more than that. Most of them seem empty but there are curtains and pots of plants at some windows.

"Let's imagine who might be living in that flat there, just above the tree, second floor, with the whitish rather transparent curtain and the green plant on the windowsill. You imagine and I will imagine, and then in a minute, we will say what we have imagined," she says.

"So, there is a single woman living in this apartment. What did you imagine?" She is ready.

"A family," he answers.

"She is single, wears expensive-looking clothes for work and spends the day in some office. She goes to the beauty salon and has colourful nails. She straightens her hair and wears lipstick for work. There's someone at the office who wants to go out with her, and this tickles her female pride; it makes her feel more powerful. She slams the kitchen cupboard doors with more confidence. And what about the family?"

"Boring. Nine to five," he replies, his cheek squashed on his hand.

"Why do you think it's boring? It depends on what's in their hearts."

"Everyone is an adventurer in their heart but they either don't…or can't live it this way," he continues gazing at the window.

"Maybe they love what they do," she suggests but is interrupted.

"I doubt it."

"Maybe she is a musician," she starts.

"And she plays for an orchestra sometimes and this is what makes everything bearable," he decides.

"Maybe she comes home inspired."

"She comes home tired."

"And what about the man?"

"He looks after the boy and stoops in front of the computer," with certainty.

"Is it a boy?"

"I think so."

"Doesn't the man work?"

"Of course."

"In front of a computer," they say in one voice.

"And he has begun to stoop, and his belly is getting soft and fat," she adds. "I'm trying to see his toenails."

"They're dirty," he says with seriousness.

She imagines them neatly cut but somehow disgusting in rubber flip-flops under the computer desk.

She suddenly goes back to the single woman living in the flat.

"But when the single woman goes out on the terrace, nothing makes her happy or sad. Her heart is shadowed, her spirit clogged. She needs to cry something out, so that she can feel joy again."

"I'm sure most of the people living in the city need this. Let's go, it's seven o'clock. We should set all the clocks according to your time, it's the right one it seems." He takes her by the hand, and they go.

To Borrow a Tulip

I took a couple of orange roses with pinkish hue to Grandpa. The best we had in the garden, the ones that grow near the apple tree. We planted the apple tree together.

I caressed the ellipse photo in golden frame on the stone and felt the emotion run through my cheeks, an instant of joy as if to meet Granddad. It didn't run to the eyes; it didn't make me cry this time, but I almost felt as if I wanted to begin speaking fast as if we hadn't seen each other for a long time. My aunt, who has a name that means 'embellish peace', started pulling the dry plants off the grave. I followed. She always speaks to him as if he is there. I usually stay silent but tell him how we are, just in my head. One of the last things I said to Granddad was that we are better than before. My aunt lit the candle. Orange roses. Some water touched the soil and disappeared. She always waters. I don't know if it's for the plants she plants or for Granddad.

The emotion is situated between my cheek bones and my eyes; it doesn't run to the lips to make them smile ('Dyado! Dyado!' I imagine myself shout and run to him, wavy hair, I'm five or so) and it doesn't run to the eyes to make them cry (I imagine the thirty-something-year-old woman angry with the indifferent and corrupted doctors, teeth clutched and bitter taste at the back of my throat). I observe both but sit still where I am now. And the emotion rises up and through my nose. But this is now, when I'm recalling the memory of me and my aunt pulling dry plants. There, engaged in careful gardening, we were calm.

As we walked out of the little graveyard of the village she told me that several months ago she borrowed a tulip from another deceased person. I looked at her with surprise and she elaborated on how she saw this grave with so many wonderful tulips and wanted to take one to 'father', so she went and asked the man whose grave flourished so colourfully. "Forgive me," she said to the invisible person and begged for a tulip 'for father'. My aunt smiled apologetically and added that she actually took two.

And then she reminded herself that she should go and take some *rakia* to the old man, in return for the tulips. She doesn't remember where exactly she borrowed the tulips, so we should wait for spring when they will be in blossom again.

Made in the USA
Monee, IL
03 May 2026

49437839R00030